SARAH AND PUFFLE

A Story for Children About Diabetes

by Linnea Mulder, R.N.

illustrated by Joanne H. Friar

Magination Press ● Washington, DC

For my daughters, Sarah and Emily, with love

I gratefully acknowledge the following people, whose efforts have made this book possible: Marilyn Milburn, R.N., for always taking the time to share her knowledge and insight gained from working with children with diabetes; Richard Mauseth, M.D., for sharing his medical knowledge and common sense views on living with a chronic illness; Carol Blainey, M.N., R.N., CDE, for sharing her practical and theoretical knowledge of diabetes; Susan Kent Cakars, Jana Johnson, Willo Davis Roberts, Suzi Tucker, and Mary K. Whittington for sharing their writing and editing gifts; Lani Kallstrom Smith, for sharing her healthy yet realistic perspective on living with diabetes; fellow members of the diabetes support group, for all you've taught me; my husband, children, and friends, for their encouragement and patience.

Library of Congress Cataloging-in-Publication Data
Mulder, Linnea.
    Sarah and Puffle : a story for children about diabetes / by Linnea Mulder ; illustrated by Joanne H. Friar.
       p. cm.
    Summary: Upset by the restrictions imposed by her diabetes, Sarah dreams about a talking sheep who helps her accept her condition.
    ISBN 0-945354-41-X. — ISBN 0-945354-42-8 (pbk.)
    [1. Diabetes—Fiction.   2. Sheep—Fiction.   3. Dreams—Fiction.]
I. Friar, Joanne H., ill. II. Title.
PZ7.M8886Sar   1992
[E]—dc20   92-25638
                                        CIP
                                        AC

Manufactured in the United States of America

10 9 8 7 6 5 4 3 2

Introduction for Parents

Approximately 120,000 children under the age of sixteen in the United States have Type 1 diabetes, also known as insulin dependent or juvenile diabetes. Type 1 diabetes is usually diagnosed in childhood, and the person is always insulin dependent. Type 2 diabetes is diagnosed during adulthood, and the person may or may not require insulin. The incidence of Type 1 diabetes is higher than most severe chronic diseases of childhood, and it appears that more children are being diagnosed with diabetes at younger ages.

When a person has diabetes, the body cannot use the food it takes in. During digestion, food breaks down into simpler forms, one of which is glucose. The pancreas produces the hormone insulin, which enables the cells to use glucose for energy. Without insulin, glucose cannot move into the cells. It builds up in the bloodstream and is excreted in the urine. The classic symptoms of diabetes onset appear: increased urination and thirst, weight loss, fatigue, nausea, and vomiting.

A person with Type 1 diabetes does not produce any or enough insulin and must get it by injection. Since it is a protein and would break down in the stomach, it cannot be taken by mouth. Insulin is necessary for survival.

No one knows what causes Type 1 diabetes. Researchers think a combination of three factors is involved: 1) an inherited susceptibility, 2) a virus or viruses, and 3) an auto-immune response in which the body destroys its own insulin–producing cells.

Type 1 diabetes is *not* caused by being overweight. It is *not* caused by eating too much sugar. It is *not* contagious. Children do not outgrow diabetes or their need for insulin. Nothing the parent or child did or did not do could have prevented the onset. Insulin does not cure diabetes, it controls it.

The management of diabetes involves more than taking shots and watching what you eat. It is a complex balance of three things: insulin dosage, exercise, and food. Growth, illness, stress, changes in activity level, changes in where shots are given, and other factors can affect this balance. On-going adjustment is needed.

Children usually have an insulin shot before breakfast and before dinner. They test their blood sugar at least two times a day. These readings help determine the amount of insulin needed. "User friendly" meters enable the young child to do all or part of this test independently.

Exercise lowers blood sugar levels and helps the body use insulin. Children can and should play actively and exercise.

Food must be eaten when insulin is working at its peak effectiveness. The meal plan usually consists of three meals and three snacks. Amounts and timing of meals need to be consistent. If not enough food is eaten, or the child exercises strenuously without a snack beforehand, an insulin reaction can occur. A child can become hungry, cranky, irritable, sweaty, shaky, or pale. Not all of these symptoms necessarily occur in young children and identifying a reaction can be difficult. Testing the blood sugar level is the only way to know for sure.

The goal of diabetes care is to have blood sugar levels as close to normal as possible. However, a child is a child first and a child with diabetes second. Blood tests, insulin shots, and food intake are not negotiable, but the details of timing and kinds of food can be. Flexibility is essential to everyone's emotional health.

So what's a parent to do? First let yourself mourn your loss and your child's loss. It is not "normal" to have shots and fingerpokes every day. It is not "normal" for families to always plan ahead, always know what time it is, always have enough food and diabetes care supplies. Don't expect perfection from yourself or your child—diabetes care has too many variables for there to be one right way to do things. Acknowledge that diabetes never takes a vacation, not even a day off. Feel sad and angry when you need to, and then move on.

Learn as much as you can. Knowledge can be gained from diabetes education classes and from your child's nurse, physician, dietician, and diabetes educator. The American Diabetes Association and the Juvenile Diabetes Foundation are national organizations aimed at promoting research and providing education. Local support groups provide a lifeline for parents. Members understand your fears and concerns. Practical tips abound. Where else can you talk about preschool and insulin reactions in the same breath?

Be proud of your child. I am humbled by my daughter's resilience and her ability to adapt to the demands of diabetes. Our children have expectations placed on them not placed on most adults. Siblings, the unsung heroes, deserve credit, too, for much is expected of them.

What can we give our children with diabetes? We can share with them what we learn. We can encourage participation in their own care. We can balance food, exercise, and insulin with common sense, love, and humor. We can listen to our children's feelings, spoken and unspoken. I hope this story can be a start.

In this story, a young child deals with some of her feelings and frustrations about having diabetes. This should offer comfort and validation to children with diabetes who have similar experiences. At the same time, basic information about the disease is introduced for all readers. On the last page of the book, a labeled diagram of a care kit shows the equipment a child with diabetes uses every day.

My daughter was diagnosed six weeks before her fourth birthday. Soon after, she asked, "Will my diabetes be over by my next birthday?" We need to support diabetes research so the answer will someday be yes. Until that time, our children can live a healthy active life with diabetes. As parents and friends, we can offer our help with their efforts, for they deserve nothing less.

Resources

American Diabetes Association
Diabetes Information Service Center, 1660 Duke Street, Alexandria, VA 22314, Tel: 800-ADA-DISC (232-3472)

Juvenile Diabetes Foundation International
120 Wall Street, 19th Floor, New York, NY 10005

Every summer Sarah and her family visited cousins who lived on a farm. They played with the lambs. They fed the ducks. They rode ponies. They ate strawberries they picked in the field. Last year was fun. But last year Sarah didn't have diabetes.

Sarah and her sister Emily galloped around the yard.

"Time to start packing," called Mother.

"Yea! Tomorrow we get to ride the pony!" shouted Emily as she raced into the house. Sarah followed slowly. She wasn't sure she wanted to go to the farm this year.

Sarah got her blue suitcase out of the closet. She packed her penguin pajamas, her purple sparkle toothbrush, her animal books. She put in some clothes and her stuffed lamb, Puffle.

"Don't forget your care kit and raisins," called her mother.

"They won't fit," said Sarah.

"Better make room," said Mother. "Remember what the doctor said about how our bodies need insulin? With diabetes, your body doesn't make insulin, so you need to get it from shots."

Sarah knew the shots kept her feeling better. She wasn't as thirsty, hungry, or tired anymore. She also remembered the nurse saying: "Too little food can make you feel hungry, shaky, and cranky. So always keep a snack with you in case you start to feel that way."

Sighing, Sarah tucked Puffle under her arm. She put the diabetes care kit and some little boxes of raisins in her suitcase.

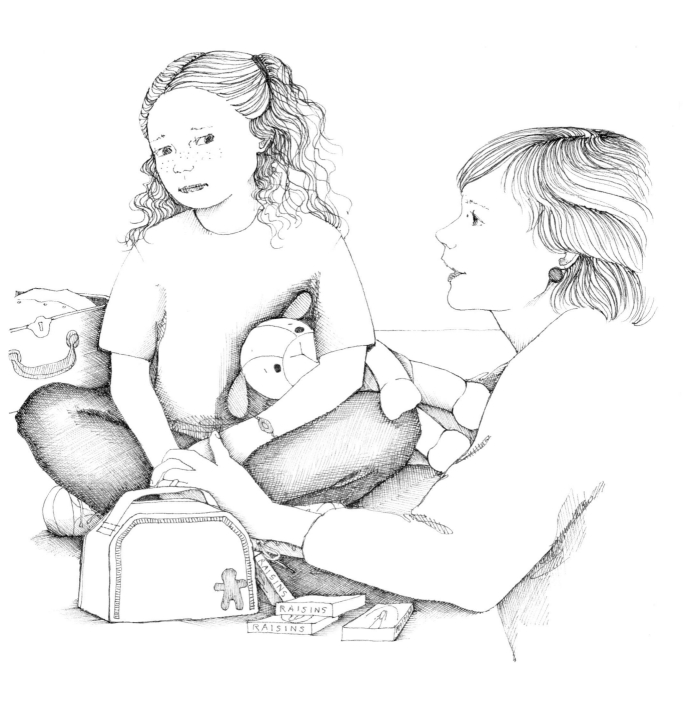

Sarah and her family left for the farm at three o'clock—snack time. In the car Sarah and Emily had animal crackers and milk. Sarah bit the head off the hippopotamus.

"Can I have more?" asked Emily.

"You can, but I can't," complained Sarah. "You can eat whatever you want whenever you want, but I have to wait for the next snack time."

"Big deal," said Emily. "You had cake and ice cream at my birthday party."

"Only because it was a special treat, and because it was snack time, and because we were riding bikes all afternoon." Sarah knew the exercise helped her body use the extra sugar.

Finally, they arrived at the farm.

"We're here!" shouted Emily.

The girls tumbled out of the car. Their cousins Brady and Jon came running to meet them.

"There's time for a pony ride before dinner," said Brady.

Sarah looked at her watch. All day long she had to know what time it was. Was it time for a snack or a blood test, a meal or an insulin shot? Stupid watch, she thought.

"Remember to be back by six o'clock for your fingerpoke and shot," said her father.

"What's a fingerpoke? asked Brady.

"Nothing," said Sarah. Her eyes suddenly filled with tears. "And I don't want a stupid pony ride."

Holding back tears, Sarah ran to the sheep pen. It's not fair, she thought. She lay down on the hay and started to cry.

"What's the matter?" asked a voice.

"Puffle, you're talking!"

"Sure am. And I'm going to the pasture. Care to join me for a walk?"

"Why were you crying?" asked Puffle.

"Because I don't want to have diabetes," said Sarah. "I'm tired of poking my finger for blood tests. I'm tired of insulin shots. I hate it when I have to stop to eat a snack when nobody else does—and when I'm not even hungry!"

"I don't blame you for feeling angry," said Puffle, "but listen . . ."

"Sarah, Sarah, are you sad?
Does diabetes make you mad?
It just happens, we don't know why.
It's not your fault; it's OK to cry."

"It rhymes!" said Sarah.
"I know," said Puffle, sheepishly.
"Do you think my diabetes will go away by my birthday?"
asked Sarah. Puffle shook his head.

"Your diabetes is here to stay.
You can't wish it or will it away.
But you can jump and skip and run—
And play with friends in the summer sun."

"Ride your bicycle, sleep in the shade,
Chomp on carrots, drink lemonade—
There are lots of things that you can do,
And some you can't, but just a few.

Sarah, Sarah, that's why I'm here,
To let you know help's always near.
Your parents, your doctor, your sister, too,
They'll do what they can, and so will you.

Tell Brady and Jon and all the folks
About insulin and fingerpokes.
Friends will like you for who you are.
Just be yourself and you'll go far."

"But none of my friends has diabetes," said Sarah.
"That's OK. Everybody's different," said Puffle.
"You're kind of different yourself," said Sarah.
"Well, baa for now." Puffle jumped over a fence, his bell jangling.

Sarah woke to the sound of the dinner bell clanging. She hurried back to the house. Emily and her cousins were already there, getting ready for dinner.

"Hey, Brady, do you still want to know about fingerpokes and insulin shots?" asked Sarah.

"Sure," said Brady.

"I have diabetes," Sarah explained, "so I have to find out how much sugar is in my blood. First I do a fingerpoke." She cleaned off her fingertip with alcohol. Then the poked herself with the lancet.

"Wow! You do that all by yourself?" asked Brady.

"Three times a day," said Sarah proudly. She squeezed a drop of blood from her fingertip and let it fall onto the test strip in the meter. "This machine tells me my blood sugar level. Then we can figure out how much insulin I need."

"Is diabetes catching?" asked Brady.

"No," said Sarah, "it isn't."

Next, Sarah's father helped her with the insulin shot.
"You're brave," said Jon.
"It doesn't hurt much," Sarah said, but secretly she agreed
with Jon.

"Come on, Sarah," said Brady, "hotdogs for supper."
"Coming," she said. Sarah put her care kit back in her suitcase.
She gave Puffle a hug. Then she ran to join the others.

Sarah's Diabetes Care Kit

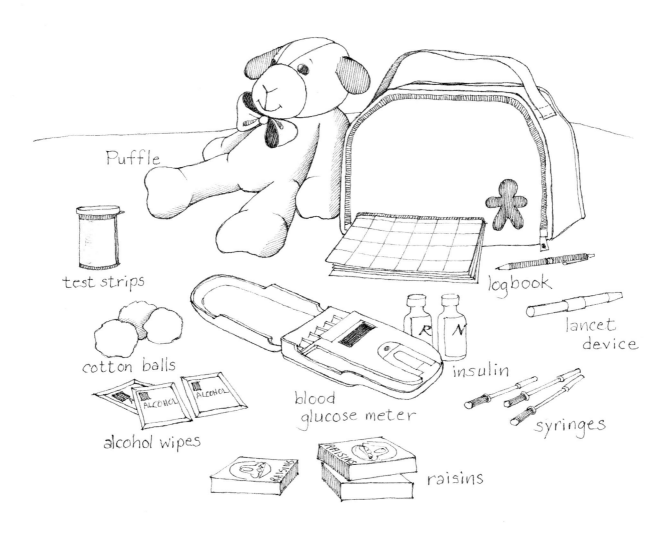

Puffle

test strips

cotton balls

alcohol wipes

blood glucose meter

logbook

insulin

raisins

lancet device

syringes